Sasha
the Slime
Fairy

By Daisy Meadows

ORCHARD

www.rainbowmagicbooks.co.uk

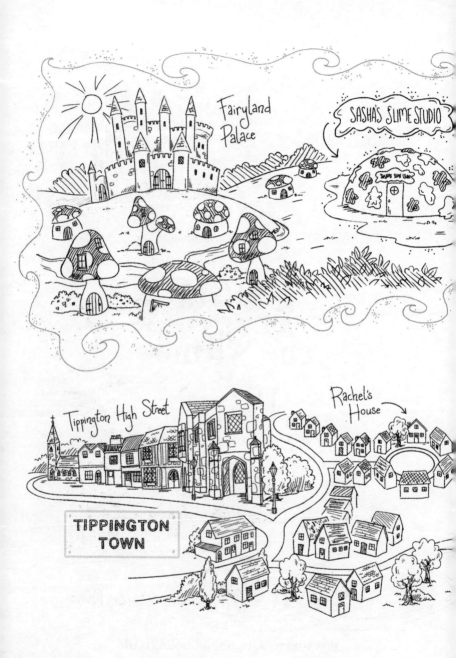

Contents

Story One:
The Glitter Slime

Story Two:
The Goo Slime

Story Three:
The Glow-in-the-Dark Slime

Jack Frost's Spell

Because the goblins won't stop shouting,
I have planned a little outing.
Off to Sasha's home I'll creep,
And steal her slime while she's asleep.

Goblins love all slime and ooze.
But fairies don't deserve to choose.
Sasha will be stopped today,
For I will take her slime away!

Story One
The Glitter Slime

Chapter One
Magical Mural

"I've never decorated a nursery school before," said Kirsty Tate.

She dipped her paintbrush into the yellow pot and started to colour the big sun on the weather wall.

"Hannah's going to love all these bright colours," said Rachel Walker.

The best friends were spending the half term in the small town of Harton, near Tippington. They were staying with Rachel's grown-up cousin Hannah, who had just opened her own nursery school. She had asked the girls to help paint a bright weather wall that would be fun for the little children.

"This looks wonderful," Hannah said, coming out of the kitchen. "Girls, I'm going to go and sort out some paperwork upstairs. When I finish, we can go for pizza, if you'd like that?"

"Yes, please!" said the girls in delight.

Hannah went up the stairs that led to her flat above the nursery school.

"Wouldn't it be amazing if we could get the whole wall finished before she comes back down?" Rachel said. "I love the green hill and the sky."

"The rain and the lightning look great too," said Kirsty. "Just the rainbow and the sun to go."

Rachel started adding purple to the rainbow she was painting, and then she stepped back in surprise.

"I've never seen paint do that before," she exclaimed.

The rainbow had started to shimmer and glow, almost as if it were real. Kirsty gave a little hop of excitement.

"It's magic," she said. "I know it is."

Kirsty and Rachel were good at spotting magic. They had shared many adventures with their secret fairy friends, taking them all over, from the turrets of the shining Fairyland Palace to the damp dungeons of Jack Frost's Castle.

"The rainbow is becoming real," Rachel whispered. "Oh my goodness, I hope that Hannah doesn't come down and see."

As they watched, the yellow arch lifted like a curtain, and a tiny fairy zoomed out, shaking silver fairy dust from her wings. She was wearing a pair of denim shorts and a cropped sleeveless shirt.

14

"Hello," she said with a confident smile. "I'm Sasha the Slime Fairy."

"It's great to meet you, Sasha," said Rachel. "I didn't even know that there was a Slime Fairy."

"That's me," said Sasha, "and I'm here to ask for your help. You see, it's my job to watch over slime makers with my special magic. I help them to have fun making and playing with slime. But this morning someone broke into my studio and smashed my jars of supplies and ingredients, so I had to cancel the slime workshops I'd planned today. Some of my ingredients have to be gathered by hand. The other fairies always say how kind and helpful you are, and I thought you might help me. Will you come to Fairyland and see if you can work out who did this horrible thing?"

"Of course we will," Kirsty said at once.

"We'd love to help," Rachel added.

"Thank you," said Sasha. "I feel better just knowing that I've got you!"

She waved her wand in a twisty pattern. A tiny golden paintbrush popped into the air beside her.

"That's pretty," said Kirsty.

Sasha smiled, and the paintbrush darted down to the bottom of the wall. With a few quick strokes it painted a tiny door with an old-fashioned key in the lock.

"Just big enough for a fairy," Rachel whispered.

Sasha gave her wand a little shake, and the painted door glowed with a golden light. Then the key turned in the lock and the door swung open.

"It's a shortcut," said Sasha. "All we have to do is fly through."

"We might need to be a little smaller," said Rachel with a giggle.

Sasha nodded and waved her wand. Instantly, a whoosh of magic ruffled the girls' hair like a sudden breeze. They shrank to fairy size, with shimmering wings as delicate as cobwebs.

"Oh my, the mural looks huge," said Kirsty.

Their hearts pitter-pattered as they fluttered towards the little door. A long curtain of rainbow-coloured beads hung in the doorway.

"Go on," said Sasha.

Kirsty went first, pushing the rainbow curtain aside. Rachel was close behind her, and she heard Kirsty gasp.

"We're here," she said, turning to smile at Rachel. "We're in Fairyland!"

Chapter Two
The Slime Studio

The rainbow bead curtain rattled as
Sasha zoomed through behind them.

"Welcome to my home," she said.

They were standing in front of a
cottage-sized cream dome, decorated
with colourful splats of slime. There was a
splat-shaped sign over the door.

Young trees were growing all around
the studio, and a little stream cut across
the corner of the garden. The water
sparkled in the sunshine.

"What an amazing place," said Rachel.

"I do love it," said Sasha. "That's why I
was so upset when I saw it this morning."

She opened the door, and Rachel and
Kirsty gasped. The studio was in an awful
mess. Jars had been smashed on the floor,
and glitter, confetti shapes, beads and
buttons were scattered everywhere. Bowls
were upside down on the tables, and
slime was dripping down the table legs.

"This is supposed to be a fun place to come," said Sasha, hanging her head. "I like it to be easy for fairies to find ingredients and have a go at making sli e. I always keep it as neat as a pin. Now look at it."

"We'll help you make it better than ever," said Rachel, putting her arm around Sasha's shoulders.

Kirsty started turning the bowls the right way up.

"Oh," she said when she picked up the last bowl. "What's this?"

Rachel and Sasha fluttered over and saw a small, blue piece of metal lying on the table. It was shaped like a lightning bolt.

"I've never seen that before," said Sasha. "Is it a brooch?"

She picked it up and held it in the palm of her hand. CRACK! The lightning bolt lit up.

"This is a message for Sasha the silly Slime Fairy," it yelled.

"Oh my goodness, it's Jack Frost's voice," said Rachel.

Sasha gasped and dropped the object on the table.

"What is a fairy doing with slime?" the voice demanded. "Slime is grim and icky and sticky and oozy and scary and MINE. It's nothing to do with a bunch of wishy-washy fairies."

"But that's ..." began Kirsty.

"Your special things belong to me now," Jack Frost boomed. "No more

slime for you."

"No!" cried Sasha.

The lightning bolt disappeared with another CRACK! and Sasha darted to the counter.

"Yes, he's taken my magical objects," she said with a groan. "What am I going to do? Without them, I can't help anyone have fun with slime."

"What are your magical objects?" Rachel asked.

"They are three special types of slime," Sasha explained. "The glitter slime makes sure that people can always find slime ingredients, wherever they live. The goo slime helps people to make the slime correctly, and the glow-in-the-dark slime makes sure that they have fun playing with it."

"So without them, no one will be able to make slime?" said Rachel, glancing at Kirsty. "My cousin Hannah was planning to make some with the older children at her nursery school tomorrow."

"I'm sorry," said Sasha. "But now that Jack Frost has my magical objects, no one will be able to make slime properly. My special magic just won't work."

Chapter Three
A Peculiar Protest

Sasha sat down on the edge of the counter and her wings drooped. Big tears brimmed in her eyes.

Kirsty and Rachel perched on the counter either side of her. They put their hands over hers.

"There is no way that Jack Frost is

getting away with this," said Kirsty in a firm voice.

"We'll go and get your things back," Rachel added. "We're not giving up."

Sasha looked amazed.

"Do you mean that you're willing to go to Jack Frost's Castle for me?" she said.

"We've been there before," said Kirsty.

"I haven't," said Sasha, shivering. "I've never even met Jack Frost."

"Will you trust us?" asked Rachel.

Sasha smiled and sat up straight. Her wings began to flutter again.

"Of course I will," she said. "Every fairy knows that you two are Fairyland's truest friends."

"Then there's no time to lose," said Kirsty. "We have to find out where Jack Frost has hidden your belongings."

"And check that he isn't plotting something mean," Rachel added.

"Just a minute," said Sasha. "I can't replace my supplies until I get the glitter slime back, but I can make things look a bit better in here."

With a wave of her wand, the broken jars and scattered supplies disappeared.

The bowls were neatly stacked up on the counter.

"This looks much better," said Kirsty. "Now, let's go and get those magical objects back."

Soon, the three fairies were zooming side by side towards the coldest corner of Fairyland.

"I see the castle," said Sasha. "It's even gloomier than I expected – like slime without colouring. Are we really going inside?"

"Yes," said Kirsty. "Jack Frost has stolen your belongings, and we'll do whatever it takes to get them back."

They got closer to the grim walls of the castle.

"Shall we slip in through the trapdoor?" Rachel asked. "I can't see any goblins

guarding it."

"Wait a minute," said Rachel. "Shh."

They stopped flying and hovered close to the battlements, listening.

"I can hear shouting," said Sasha. "Lots of shouting."

Slowly, the fairies fluttered around the side of the castle. A small group of goblins was standing outside the castle.

They were waving banners and placards, and squawking up at one of the castle windows.

"Slime for the slimy!"

"Fairies with slime, what a crime!"

"Goblins have rights too!"

"Look," said Kirsty. "Jack Frost is leaning out of the castle window."

"Rubbish," bawled Jack Frost, shaking his fist at the goblins. "The only right you nincompoops have is the right to stop shouting!"

"But we're fed up with the fairies having slime," the goblins whined. "They shouldn't enjoy making it or playing with it."

"They can't any more," bellowed Jack Frost. "Thanks to me, that pesky fairy will never make slime again. Here, take this and leave me alone. I'm fed up with all the noise. I've been up all night and I need my beauty sleep."

He hurled something at the goblins, and then disappeared back into the castle.

"What did he throw?" Rachel asked.

"I couldn't tell," said Kirsty. "It was small and white – that's all I saw."

"Small and white with tiny sparkles all over it," said Sasha in a miserable voice. "I'd know it anywhere. It's my glitter slime."

Chapter Four
The Goblin Village

"We've found the glitter slime," said Rachel, delighted.

"But it's getting away again," Kirsty added. "Come on."

The goblins were already halfway along the winding path that led to their village. They were skipping and

whooping, tossing the glitter slime
between them. None of them noticed
that they were being followed by three
fairies.

"How are we going to fly through
Goblin Grotto without being seen?"
Sasha asked.

"I've got an idea," said Rachel. "As

soon as we get to the village, can you turn us into something really small? Then we can follow the glitter slime and take it back as soon as the goblins are looking the other way."

"I can do that," said Sasha. "I just hope that we get the chance to take the glitter slime back."

Ahead, they could see the roofs of the huts that the goblins called home. Other goblins were calling and waving to those with the glitter slime.

"Now," Rachel whispered. "Time for a little disguise."

Sasha waved her wand, and the girls suddenly felt their arms and legs shrinking. Their wings were becoming stubby.

"My body's getting wider," said Kirsty,

laughing. "And I think I've got extra legs. Sasha, what are we turning into?"

"You'll see," said Sasha, laughing.

In another moment, three tiny ladybirds flew into Goblin Grotto, close behind the goblin who was carrying the glitter slime.

"That was a wonderful spell," said Rachel.

"I can't stop giggling," said Sasha, panting. "It's just so funny trying to fly with these tiny little wings."

"I keep wiggling my antennae," Kirsty added. "It's a nice, tickly sort of feeling."

After a few minutes, they reached the main square, and at that moment the goblins darted into a large hut.

"They've left the door open," said Rachel. "Come on, we have to go inside and find out what they're doing. Maybe we can talk to them and persuade them to give the glitter slime back."

The three ladybird-fairies followed the goblins into the hut. The first thing they noticed was the noise. The squawking, shouting, groaning and grumbling was so loud that it made them want to fly away.

"Can you see the goblins?" Kirsty shouted.

Rachel and Sasha didn't hear her. They gazed around the room. There were long tables piled high with broken crayons, torn pieces of cardboard and rough planks of wood. Most goblins were squabbling, but a few were writing on the cardboard and gluing it to the wood.

"They're making placards," said Rachel in astonishment.

There were lots of placards piled up in the corner.

Slime's too good for fairies!

Grotty slime belongs in Goblin Grotto!

Fairies, forget slime!

"What did Jack Frost say?" a goblin

called out.

Another goblin jumped on to a table, holding the glitter slime.

"Jack Frost told us that the fairies won't be able to play with slime any more," he yelled. "We've won!"

He threw the glitter slime down on

the glue table and it made a loud splat. The others capered around, cackling with laughter and cheering.

"We're never going to persuade them to give back the glitter slime," said Rachel. "Just look at all these placards. They won't want to hear anything about fairies."

"That's given me an idea," said Kirsty.
"I think I know how to distract them."

Chapter Five
Distraction!

"Sasha, you'll need to turn us back into fairies again," said Kirsty.

"But what if we're seen?" Sasha asked with a gasp.

"We'll hide under the tables," said Kirsty. "Come on."

She dived downwards and Rachel and

Sasha followed her. As soon as they were under the table, Sasha turned them all back into fairies.

"What's your plan?" Rachel asked her best friend.

"Get a piece of cardboard and start writing some new placards," said Kirsty. "But these ones are going to be nice about fairies. If we can get the goblins to notice them, maybe they'll be so busy complaining that we can reach the glitter slime without them seeing."

There were lots of crayon pieces and cardboard squares on the floor.

"For once it's a good thing that that the goblins are so messy," said Rachel.

She and Kirsty wrote on every piece of card that they could find. Soon they had a pile of placards. Sharing a hopeful

smile, they pushed the pieces of card out from under the table.

"Fingers crossed," Kirsty whispered.

The placards bumped into the feet of the nearest goblin, and he looked down.

"What's this?" he squawked. "Hey, which pea-brain wrote these?"

The other goblins looked too, and started reading out the words that the fairies had written.

"Fairies love slime."

"Slime for everyone."

"Share the slime."

"Fairies are our friends."

For a moment, the goblins stared at each other in amazement. Then a huge hullabaloo broke out.

"Who wrote this?"

"Own up – was it you?"

The goblins yelled and pointed their bony fingers at each other. One broke a placard over another's head. They argued and shouted and squawked. Not one of them was looking at the glue table.

"We have to make a dash for it," said Kirsty.

"I'm nervous," said Sasha.

"We're together," said Rachel, taking her hand. "There's nothing we can't do."

"Ready?" Kirsty whispered. "Now."

Faster than arrows, the fairies sped towards the glue table.

"Fairies!" yelled the goblin closest to

them. "Get them!"

Kirsty stretched her hand out towards the glitter slime. The goblins dived towards them.

"Faster," Sasha cried.

Kirsty's fingers closed around the slime, and Sasha instantly waved her wand. There was a burst of fairy dust, and then they were once more standing outside Sasha's studio.

"Oh my goodness, that was close," said Sasha, her hand over her heart. "I'm sure a goblin touched my wing."

"But he didn't catch you," said Rachel. "And you've got your glitter slime back. Hurray!"

"This means I can magic up some new slime ingredients for my studio," said Sasha. "Thank you, Rachel and Kirsty. It's all because of you."

"We're so glad we could help," said
Kirsty.

Rachel pointed to the rainbow bead
curtain, which was still hanging in the air
opposite the studio.

"It's time for us to get back to Harton," she said. "But please come and find us when you've got all your ingredients back. We won't give up until all your magical objects are back where they belong!"

Story Two
The Goo Slime

Chapter Six
The Struggle With Slime

"Welcome to the slime surgery!" said Kirsty.

"We'll try to answer all your slime questions," Rachel added.

They smiled at the mum and little boy who had just arrived at Hannah's nursery-school slime event. Lots of children were already inside with their parents. Hannah came over to stand beside the girls.

"Thanks for helping," she said. "Oh my goodness, I hope today is a success."

"I'm sure it will be," Rachel told her cousin. "You've worked so hard to make everything perfect."

Hannah smiled at her.

"Thanks," she said. "You're right, I have worked hard, so there's no reason for anything to go wrong."

As she walked away, the best friends exchanged a worried glance. They knew that there was one extremely good reason why things might go wrong. Jack Frost and his mischievous  goblins still had two of Sasha's magical objects. Without them, slime-makers all over the world would be disappointed.

"I hope that we can find the goo slime

and the glow-in-the-dark slime soon," Rachel whispered.

"We can't do much until Sasha comes and finds us," said Kirsty. "For now, let's focus on helping your cousin."

The nursery was soon full of people, and Hannah clapped her hands together. Everyone stopped talking.

"Thank you all for coming," Hannah said. "It's great to see so many people here, and I hope you like my new nursery school. I've opened up today so that parents can look around, and because everyone loves slime – right?"

All the children cheered, and Hannah laughed.

"But not everyone knows how to make it," she went on. "Today will change all that. On each table you will find a different slime recipe and all the ingredients you'll need. So pick a table and get stuck in!"

The excited chatter broke out again as people chose their tables.

"Hannah has labelled each table with the kind of slime you can make there," said Rachel, reading the labels aloud.

"Classic slime, sparkle slime, mood slime, crunchy slime, mermaid slime, toxic slime … I didn't know that there were so many different types!"

"And greedy Jack Frost wants to keep it all to himself," said Kirsty.

"It isn't Jack Frost being greedy this time," Rachel reminded her. "It's the goblins who want to stop fairies from enjoying the fun of slime. I've been thinking about it, and I think Jack Frost stole Sasha's magical objects so that the goblins would stop bothering him by moaning about it. I think that they care more about the slime than Jack Frost does."

Just then, the girls noticed Hannah beckoning to them. They hurried over to see what she wanted.

"Could you go round and help anyone who's stuck?" she asked.

The girls nodded and looked around. Parents and children were poring over the instructions together. The chatter had become a mumble at almost every table. The odd ones out were a loud family who were squabbling over the instructions.

"Add the food colouring first," the little boy shouted.

"No, the glue first," yelled his dad, who was wearing a long, flowing coat. "I'm supposed to be the grown-up."

"That's an unusual thing for a grown-up to say," Rachel murmured.

TOXIC SLIME

"They're both a bit unusual," said Kirsty. "They're wearing the same caps. It's almost as if—"

"Excuse me, could you help me?" asked a little girl. "My slime is too sticky."

"We'll take a look," said Rachel.

They followed the little girl, forgetting all about the unusual family.

Chapter Seven
Knock Knock!

For the next ten minutes, Rachel and Kirsty thought only about slime. Everyone seemed to need them.

"This slime is too runny," a little boy wailed.

"There's probably not enough starch," said Kirsty, hurrying to help.

"This slime has gone hard," cried a small girl.

"You need a bit more water," said Rachel. "Let me show you."

But although the girls did all the right things, not a single slime recipe worked. Hannah was having the same trouble. She darted from group to group wearing a worried frown.

"Perhaps we should throw all the mixtures away and start again," said one of the parents.

"You might be right," said Hannah, groaning.

Just then, the family in caps started cackling with laughter.

"It works!" squawked the little boy.

He lifted handfuls of bright-green slime and let it ooze through his fingers.

"Goodness, your slime is perfect," Hannah exclaimed. "Perhaps we should let you teach everyone the recipe."

"I'm busy," snapped the little boy. "Why should I help them?"

"He's as rude as a goblin," said Kirsty.

As soon as she said the word 'goblin', she realised the truth. So did Rachel. The best friends exchanged a horrified glance.

"That 'family' isn't a family at all," Rachel whispered in alarm. "They're goblins. Somehow, that parent goblin has made himself look tall. I bet they've got Sasha's goo slime. That's how they've made it so perfect."

"We have to tell Sasha," said Kirsty.

"But how?"

Rachel tapped the locket that was hidden under her T-shirt. Queen Titania had given one to each girl, and the fairy dust inside was enough for one trip to Fairyland. But Kirsty shook her head.

"It's no use," she said. "We can't use fairy magic in front of all these people."

They glanced around the room. Most of the parents and children were still trying to make their slime work. At that

74

moment, the goblin
parent snatched some
of the slime and
threw it at the mural.

"Please don't do
that," said Hannah in
a surprised voice.

Rachel stared at the
slime dripping down
the mural they had
painted the day before.

"That gives me an idea," she said as
the goblins cackled with laughter. "What
about the fairy door on the mural? Sasha
said that it's a shortcut to Fairyland, and
it comes out at her studio. If we knock on
it hard enough, maybe she'll hear us."

"Great idea," said Kirsty.

They hurried over to the mural. At

the bottom was the tiny fairy door that
Sasha's magic paintbrush had made.
Rachel stood in front of it and Kirsty
knelt down. She knocked hard several
times.

"Is the door glowing?" Rachel
whispered. "Can you see anything
magical happening?"

"No," said Kirsty with a sigh.

She turned away and
bumped into the goblin
parent. He staggered
sideways, and a wide,
green foot poked out
from halfway up his
coat. He shoved it back
in again, but Rachel
and Kirsty had spotted
it.

"You're not one
goblin," Rachel said
in a low voice. "You're
two – one on top of the
other."

A look of panic crossed the goblin's
face. He stuck out his tongue and then
turned and hurried back to his table. He
whispered to the little-boy goblin, who

pointed to the door.

"They're leaving," said Kirsty. "We have to stop them."

The goblins gathered their slime into a bucket and headed towards the door. But before the girls could follow them, Rachel noticed something among the slime ingredients on Hannah's desk.

"Kirsty, look at the starry glitter pot," she squeaked. "It's glowing."

They dashed over and peered into the pot. The starry glitter was moving and swirling into a familiar shape … a shape with tiny, fluttering wings. It was Sasha!

Chapter Eight
Slime Attack!

"I heard you knocking," said Sasha.
"What a clever way to reach me! I
guessed you wanted me to come."

"The goblins are here," Kirsty gabbled.
"We think they have the goo slime."

"Their slime was perfect and no one
else's worked," Rachel added.

"And they're leaving," said Kirsty. "Come on."

Sasha slipped into Rachel's dress pocket, and the girls darted over to Hannah.

"We think we might be able to make the slime work better, but we have to go out for a little while," said Rachel. "Is that OK?"

"Yes, of course," said Hannah, looking anxious. "If you know a way to save the slime surgery, please try."

Rachel and Kirsty ran out of the nursery and saw three goblins dart into a lane halfway along the road. The parent goblin had split in two, and the one who

had been on top now had a long coat
dragging on the ground.

"That lane goes to the play park," said
Rachel. "We can catch up with them
there."

The girls sped down the lane and into
the play park. At once, something green
hurtled past Kirsty's head and hit a tree
with a loud SPLAT!

"Duck!" cried Kirsty.

They dived behind the slide. THUD!

"They're throwing slime bombs at us," Rachel exclaimed.

WHUMP! Another slime bomb hit the slide and splashed Kirsty's shoes.

"Run for the seesaw," she said.

As they ran, they saw the three goblins sitting on the swings, passing the bucket between them and sniggering.

"Slime fight!" they shouted.

Rachel and Kirsty ran towards the roundabout, ducking and dodging as slime bombs shot past their ears. Sasha popped her head out of Rachel's pocket.

"Let's get closer to them," Sasha said. "We have to find out where they're keeping the goo slime. Without it, no one will ever be able to make slime again."

The goblins squawked and jabbered at the girls.

"Stand still and be splatted!"

"They're friends with the fairies!"

"Don't trust them!"

Rachel and Kirsty clambered over the climbing frame and swung across the

monkey bars. Slime bombs whizzed past them.

"Please stop throwing slime at us," Rachel called. "We want to talk to you."

The goblins paused, their hands poised

over their bucket.

"We don't care what you say," squawked the goblin in the long coat.

"The goo slime doesn't belong to you," said Kirsty. "Please give it back."

The goblin curled his lip.

"Why does she want it?" shouted the little-boy goblin. "Fairies shouldn't like slime."

"Why?" asked Rachel.

"Because fairies are fluffy and fluttery and pretty," said the goblin in the coat. "If you look like a fairy, you have to like disgusting pink, frilly things. It's the rule."

At that, Sasha shot out of Rachel's pocket and hovered in front of the goblins.

"That's the silliest thing I've ever heard," she said, folding her arms. "I'm a fairy and I love slime. It's fun."

"No, goblins and fairies are different!" the third goblin

screeched crossly.

"You're right," said Kirsty in a calm voice. "But they're different because of what they do, not how they look."

"Just because someone looks pretty and delicate, it doesn't mean they're not strong and brave," Rachel went on.

"And it doesn't mean that they're not allowed to like slime," added Sasha.

"Hogwash," snarled the goblin in the coat.

"Sasha can prove it," said Kirsty. "You could look like a fairy and still feel like a goblin inside."

Sasha waved her wand, and the goblins were showered with fairy dust.

Chapter Nine
Fairy Goblins

When the sparkles cleared, three green
fairies were fluttering over the bucket of
slime.

"Ha ha, look at you two!" cackled the
little-boy goblin. "You're fairies!"

Then he looked down and his face
went pale green.

"Oh no, I'm a fairy," he squealed.

"That's disgusting!"

"Now that you look like fairies, have you stopped liking slime?" asked Sasha.

"No, of course not," the goblin in the coat yelled, fluttering his gauzy wings. "No way."

"You see?" said Sasha. "It's who you are on the inside that counts."

With a hopeful smile, she raised her

wand and POP! The goblins were back to normal.

"Ugh, that was horrible," said the third goblin, wiping his forehead. "It'll give me nightmares."

"Now you can see why I need my goo slime back," said Sasha. "I don't look like you, but I love slime just as much as you do."

"No you don't," the goblins shouted, closing their eyes and sticking their fingers in their ears. "You're never getting it back. La la la!"

Sasha looked sad, but Rachel had an idea.

"I think I know a way to make them

show us where the goo slime is," she said
quickly.

She rummaged around in her pocket

and pulled something
out, cupped in her hands.
Then she started to jump
up and down.

"The goo slime!" she
shouted at the top of her
voice. "The goo slime!"

The goblins heard her.
They opened their eyes
and leapt to their feet.

"She's got it!" wailed
the one in the coat.

In a panic, the little-boy goblin tore the
cap off his head and peered inside.

"It's still here," he said, glaring at
Rachel and jamming the cap back on his

head. "You haven't got
it."

"But now I know
where it is," said
Rachel.

"You tricked me!"
the goblin screeched.

"I didn't say I had it,"
said Rachel, truthfully.

The goblin stamped his feet and waved
his fists at her.

"You're letting your temper take
control," said Kirsty. "Please try to calm
down."

"Shut up!" the goblin shouted. "Slime
bomb!"

He grabbed the bucket of slime, but it
was empty.

"Please listen," said Rachel. "Sasha

95

knows how to make all kinds of slime.
She could magic up buckets and buckets
of slime for you. All you have to do is
give her back the goo slime."

The goblin grabbed a handful of grass
and hurled it at Rachel.

"Go away!" he bellowed, looking
around for something else to throw.

The other goblins joined in, throwing

twigs, gravel and handfuls of soil. Then
the goblin in the coat yanked his hat off
and sent it spinning towards the girls like
a Frisbee.

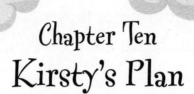

Chapter Ten
Kirsty's Plan

The cap hit Kirsty's shoulder hard.

"Ouch!" she cried.

The goblins cackled with laughter.

"I've got an idea," Kirsty whispered.
"Goblins don't like being told what to
do. Maybe if I try to boss the goblin
around, it will make him so cross that

he'll do the exact opposite."

She looked at the little-boy goblin and put her hands on her hips.

"Don't you dare copy him and throw your cap at me," she called out. "Don't you dare!"

At once, the goblin snatched the cap off his head and hurled it towards the girls with all his strength.

"Yes!" cried Kirsty.

She leapt into the air and caught it with one hand. At that moment, the goblin realised what he had done.

"The goo slime!" he squawked. "NO!"

The other two goblins turned on him, waving their arms around and shouting.

"People make silly choices when their temper is in charge," said Kirsty. "And so do goblins!"

She reached into the hat and pulled out a small, shimmering pot.

"The goo slime!" Sasha exclaimed.

As soon as she touched it, the pot of goo slime shrank to fairy size.

"Hurray!" cried Sasha, turning a somersault in the air. "Thank you, Rachel and Kirsty!"

The girls laughed happily as the little fairy turned another somersault, gave them a cheery wave and then vanished in a starburst of fairy dust.

Hand in hand, Rachel and Kirsty ran
back to Hannah's nursery school. Even
before they went in, they could hear
happy laughter and delighted squeals.

"There you are," said Hannah as they
dashed back in. "You'll never believe it.
We were about to throw the slime away,
and then all of a sudden it started to
work. Look!"

Around the room, children were stirring
extra ingredients into their buckets. Beads
were being added for crunchy slime, as
well as buttons, foam and glitter of every
colour. Meanwhile the parents were
looking around the nursery at all the
things Hannah had set up.

"This is great," said Rachel. "I bet some of these mums and dads will want their children to come here next term."

Hannah crossed her fingers and grinned at them.

"I really hope so," she said. "I've dreamed of running my own nursery school for years."

She went to chat to the parents, and Rachel and Kirsty shared a happy hand squeeze.

"We did it," Rachel said. "There's just one more magical object to find."

"And we're going to find it," said Kirsty in a determined voice. "We won't let those goblins spoil things for Sasha."

"And we'll do everything we can to make Hannah's dream come true," Rachel added. "But first, let's go and make some slime of our own!"

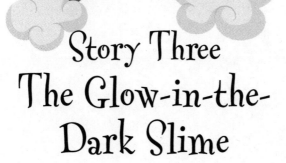

Story Three
The Glow-in-the-
Dark Slime

Chapter Eleven
Frozen Slime

"Let's make this batch of slime sparkly," said Rachel, tipping a tub of glitter into the bucket.

Kirsty stirred the glitter into their bright-orange slime and giggled.

"This looks great," she said. "Thank goodness we helped Sasha find the goo slime. Making slime is so much fun."

"Don't forget to play with it," said Hannah, laughing as she passed their table.

Around them, there were still plenty of children following instructions to make slime. Hannah was busy helping them and answering questions from their parents about her new nursery school.

"Hannah's right," said Rachel, looking around at the other children. "Everyone's so busy making slime that they're forgetting to actually play with it."

Kirsty gasped, her hand to her mouth.

"Oh my goodness," she said. "I'd forgotten about what Sasha's third magical object does."

Sasha had told them that the glow-in-the-dark slime made sure that people had fun playing with slime.

"The funny thing is, I can't quite remember how to play with slime either," said Rachel.

"It's easy," said Kirsty. "You just … we … er … I don't know."

The girls sat and stared at the glittery orange slime. Then Rachel glanced at the mural and gasped. The little door that Sasha's magic paintbrush had

painted was glowing.

"Look, Kirsty," she began – but she was interrupted.

CRASH! The nursery school door burst open.

"Oh no," said Kirsty.

Jack Frost was standing in the doorway with the three goblins who had been at

the slime surgery earlier.

"That's them," the goblins squawked, pointing at Rachel and Kirsty. "Teach them a lesson."

Jack Frost raised his wand and there was a tremendous crack of lightning. At exactly the same moment, the girls heard a tinkling sound, as if hundreds of tiny bells were ringing. When they looked around, they saw that everyone in the nursery school had stopped moving. Hannah's hand was up by her ear, halfway through flicking her hair back. The girl beside her was still too, with purple slime stretched between her hands. Behind them, two of the parents were frozen halfway through a conversation.

"It's as if someone pressed 'pause' on a film," said Rachel in amazement.

"What have you done?" exclaimed Kirsty, turning to Jack Frost.

"Why aren't you frozen?" he roared.

They heard the tinkling sound again, and then Sasha fluttered out from behind a table. She looked nervous but determined.

"They are my friends, and they are

protected by fairy dust," she said, bravely.

"The fairy dust in our lockets must have protected us from the spell," Kirsty whispered.

They watched as Sasha pointed her wand at the door. It swung shut, and they heard the lock click.

"Now no one can come in and see what's happening here," she said. "It gives us time to put this right."

"Sasha, are these people hurt?" Rachel asked.

The fairy shook her head.

"Jack Frost has frozen bubbles of time around everyone in here," she said. "For them, time is standing still. They aren't in any

117

danger, but this is fairy magic. Jack Frost must be using the magical power of the glow-in-the-dark slime."

"That means it's nearby," said Kirsty. "But where?"

Chapter Twelve
Stuck in the Slime

Jack Frost had been listening to Sasha. He gave them all a mean grin.

"You'll never get the glow-in-the-dark slime," he said. "I'm too clever for you and I've chosen a super-clever hiding place that you will never find, even if you search the whole nursery school from top to bottom."

Rachel turned to Kirsty in excitement.

"That means it's somewhere in the nursery school," she said.

"Rats!" growled Jack Frost, clenching his fists.

"Tee hee," the goblins giggled. "Jack Frost is a silly billy. Now they know it's in the messy-play room."

"Nitwits!" Jack Frost roared. "Now they know where to look!"

The girls raced towards the messy-play room at the back of the nursery school, and Sasha zoomed after them.

"Stop them!" squealed the smallest goblin.

"Switch your brain on," Jack Frost said. "I've used the power of the glow-in-the-dark slime to make booby traps. They'll

never beat me."

"My magical slime isn't meant to be used to make booby traps," cried Sasha. "It's supposed to help people have fun playing with slime."

"I'm having fun," cackled Jack Frost.

Just as Rachel and Kirsty reached the door of the messy-play room, something strange happened. One moment they were sprinting, and the next moment …

"My feet are stuck," said Rachel.

They looked down and gasped.

"The floor has turned to slime," said Kirsty with a groan. "Sticky slime."

Jack Frost swaggered up to the edge of the slime. He clicked his fingers and a tub of popcorn appeared in his hand.

"I'm going to enjoy seeing you stuck," he said.

Sasha fluttered around the girls, clasping her hands together.

"I'm sorry, but I can't help you," she said. "Jack Frost has used my glow-in-the-dark slime to make it, so I won't be able to magic it away."

Rachel looked around and spotted a broom leaning against the wall.

"Kirsty, can you reach that?" she asked, pointing. "Maybe we can use it to pull ourselves out.

Kirsty stretched out her hand as far as she could. Her fingertips brushed the broom handle and it clattered to the ground. Hooking the brush under a chair, Kirsty managed to pull one foot out of the sticky slime. The other came out with a loud squelch.

"Give me your hand," said Kirsty, reaching out to her best friend.

With some strong pulling and the help of the broom, Rachel was free. The girls sat at the edge of the slime, catching their breath. At that moment, the slime disappeared and the floor was a floor again.

"Quickly," said Sasha, fluttering down beside them. "Let me turn you into fairies before he can turn the floor into slime again."

She waved her wand and a swirl of fairy dust instantly appeared. It started at the girls' feet and then whirled up around them, shrinking them to fairy size.

"Hurray for wings!' said Kirsty, laughing as she fluttered them. "There is

nothing as beautiful as fairy wings."

Rachel and Kirsty swooped into the air beside Sasha.

"Now, into the messy-play room," Rachel said.

Jack Frost threw his popcorn down and

folded his arms.

"You won't find it as easily as you think," he said.

Chapter Thirteen
A Slimy Trap

Jack Frost snapped his fingers, and the goblins raced over with buckets of slime. Jack Frost sent a bolt of blue lightning shooting at the buckets.

"Hee hee," the goblins squawked.

They plunged their bony hands into the buckets and pulled out handfuls of purple slime.

"Oh my goodness, the slime is moving," cried Kirsty.

"It's squiggling," the goblins screeched. "Get them!"

The goblins hurled handful after handful of wriggling slime worms into the air. The fairies dived and dodged out of the way.

"Slime bombs are horrible when we're human-sized," Rachel panted. "But if they hit us now we're fairies, they could really hurt."

The slime worms coiled as they flew upwards. It was as if they were trying to catch the fairies.

"We have to get into the messy-play room and shut the door," Kirsty called out.

When the goblins heard that, they threw even more slime worms, harder and harder. The fairies were forced away from the messy-play room. They darted into the lampshade to hide.

Rachel tried to catch her breath.

"I've got an idea," she said. "Sasha, I know that you can't change the slime without all three of your magical objects, but you can change us. If you could make us look like the slime worms, we might be able to slip into the messy-play room without the goblins realising."

Sasha's eyes sparkled with the fun of the idea. With a wave of her wand, all three of them turned purple. Their bodies stretched until they looked exactly like the wiggly worms that the goblins were throwing.

"Quickly, the magic won't last long," Sasha called out.

The goblins were still throwing slime into the air in a half-hearted way.

"I can't see them," the tallest goblin wailed. "I want to stop throwing now. My arm hurts."

None of them noticed three purple worms gliding across the ceiling. They

zoomed through the doorway of the messy-play room just as they turned back into fairies.

"Phew," said Kirsty, peeping around the door. "The goblins don't know we're in here. They're still throwing slime worms around."

Rachel and Sasha gazed around the messy-play room.

"Oh my goodness, there are so many places where the slime could be hidden," said Sasha. "Where shall we start?"

The fairies flew around the room, looking this way and that. They peered into jars of pom-poms and lolly sticks. They searched among bottles of poster paint and sticks of glue.

"Nothing," said Rachel with a groan. "If the glow-in-the-dark slime is in here,

Jack Frost must have found a really good hiding place."

At that moment, a goblin skidded into the room and stopped right in front of them. His eyes opened very wide.

"They're here!" he squawked.

The other goblins ran in too, followed by Jack Frost. He shoved the goblins aside and grinned at the fairies.

"You fell into my trap," he said, raising his wand. "I told the goblins to lie about the hiding place. I told them to say the slime was here in the messy-play room. Fools! You've been tricked, and now you will be trapped in here for ever!"

Chapter Fourteen
Slime Surfers

There was a loud rumbling sound. Then Kirsty turned around and gasped. Behind them, a long wave of slime was rising up from the floor, getting higher and higher.

"This isn't what slime is for," Rachel said. "You're just a big bully, Jack Frost!"

Jack Frost cackled with laughter, and

held up a handful of glowing slime.

"My glow-in-the-dark slime!" Sasha cried.

Then Jack Frost and the goblins vanished in a flash of blue lightning.

"The wave is going to crash down on us," Rachel shouted. "There's no time to fly out of the way."

"Sasha, let's go slime surfing!" Kirsty exclaimed.

With a flick of Sasha's wand, three surfboards appeared on the very top of the wave. The fairies flew up to them and jumped on just in time. CRASH! The slime wave plunged across the messy-play room, and the fairies surfed ahead of it.

"Woo-hoo!" Rachel cheered, laughing. "This is amazing fun!"

Balancing on the surfboards, the fairies

wobbled and giggled as they sped along.
At last the wave died down, and the
surfboards came to rest at the back of the
messy-play room.

"That was quick thinking, Kirsty," said
Sasha.

"What shall we do now?" Rachel

asked. "Jack Frost has disappeared."

"I'll bet he's gone straight back to his castle," said Kirsty. "He's been so busy thinking about playing his trick on us, he won't have thought of another place to hide the slime."

"Then let's go to the Ice Castle," said Sasha.

With a wave of her wand, the walls of the messy-play room seemed to melt away. The fairies were hovering outside a window of Jack Frost's castle.

"It's open," said Rachel, darting forwards.

They slipped through the window and found themselves in a long, thin corridor.

"I've never seen anything like it," said Sasha.

Kirsty and Rachel had been to the castle many times, so they weren't surprised. They were used to the thick cobwebs that hung in every corner. They had seen the damp walls and felt the chill in the air. The torch lamp on the wall flickered.

"How are we ever going to find the slime in this huge castle?" Sasha asked.

The torch lamp flickered again. Then a cold blast of air whooshed down the corridor and blew out the light.

"Brrr," said Kirsty, rubbing her arms. "It feels colder than ever today."

"Follow me," Rachel whispered. "I

remember this corridor. It leads to the throne room. "

The fairies flew down the corridor to the door of the throne room. It was half open and they peeped in.

"Goodness, I've never seen so many goblins," said Kirsty. "Or so much slime."

"It looks as if Jack Frost is holding his own slime surgery," said Rachel.

The throne room was filled with goblins, all standing at tables filled with slime ingredients. Slime was dripping off the tables and oozing across the floor. Goblins squelched through it and plunged their arms into it. Slime dripped from the ceiling and splatted on bony green heads.

"Look, Jack Frost is on his throne," Sasha whispered.

Jack Frost was cackling with laughter

as he watched the goblins get messier and messier.

"He has my magical slime somewhere

in there," said Sasha. "But how can we search for it in a room full of goblins?"

Chapter Fifteen
Stop That Slime!

"I have an idea," said Rachel in excitement. "Remember how the wind blew the torch lamp out? What if Sasha made the throne room go dark? Maybe we could spot the glow-in-the-dark slime."

"Can you do that?" Kirsty asked,

turning to the Slime Fairy.

"The curtains are closed, and it's gloomy outside," said Sasha, nodding. "I can make it dark enough."

She flicked her wand at the lights in the throne room. One by one, they flickered out.

"What's going on?" Jack Frost roared.

The goblins squealed and squawked. They were so loud that they didn't hear Rachel cry out, "There!"

On the floor beside Jack Frost's throne, something was glowing yellowy-orange in the darkness.

"That's it," Sasha whispered. "But how can we get it in the dark, with all those goblins in the way?"

"I'll do it," said Kirsty. "I think it would be better for just one of us to go."

"It looks scary," said Sasha. "Are you sure?"

Kirsty hugged her, and then swooped into the room. She flew high until she

was over the glowing slime. Then she carefully fluttered down, taking care to avoid the goblins. Luckily, they had all crouched down with their bottoms in the air and their hands over their heads. No one saw Kirsty land beside the slime. But when it rose into the air with her, Jack Frost howled.

"Stop that slime!" he yelled. "It's flying!"

But he was too late. The slime whizzed through the air and Kirsty placed it safely in Sasha's hand.

"Yes!" Sasha exclaimed.

She waved her wand, and there was a fizzy, sparkling puff of fairy dust. When it cleared, the three fairies were standing outside Sasha's Slime Studio. Sasha threw her arms around Rachel and Kirsty.

"You are wonderful friends," she said.

"Because of you, all three of my magical objects are back where they belong. Thank you from the bottom of my heart."

"We're so happy that things are put right," said Kirsty, smiling.

"And slime will be fun for everyone again," Rachel added.

Kirsty glanced at the rainbow-coloured bead curtain.

"Is that still a shortcut to the nursery school?" she asked.

Sasha fluttered over and held the strings of beads aside.

"Oh, what about Jack Frost's freezing spell?" Rachel asked, suddenly remembering how they had left the nursery school.

"Now all my slime has been found, everything will be back to normal," Sasha said. "But I hope you will visit me through the magical door whenever you stay with your cousin."

The fairies shared a hug, and then Rachel and Kirsty stepped through the curtain. In a flash, they had grown to human size, and they were standing beside a table of slime.

"Everything is going so well," said Hannah, squeezing Rachel's shoulder as she passed. "Thank you for all your help

getting the nursery school ready."

"It's been fun to help," said Rachel.

"And the slime surgery has been the most fun of all," added Kirsty. "In fact,

I'm sure people are going to think that your new nursery school is absolutely magical!"

The End

Now it's time for Kirsty and Rachel to help …

Ivy the Worry Fairy

Read on for a sneak peek …

"I can't believe we're both here," said Rachel Walker.

"Me neither," said her best friend, Kirsty Tate. "It was the best surprise ever when we arrived last night and saw you."

It was Saturday morning, and the girls were looking forward to a relaxing weekend at the Olive House Family Mindfulness Retreat.

"Our parents are pretty good at keeping secrets," said Rachel, laughing. "They planned for us to be here together, and they didn't say a word about it."

The girls shared a very special secret of their own. Ever since they had first met, they had been friends with the fairies. They had been to Fairyland many times, and were always ready to help the fairies foil bad-tempered Jack Frost and his naughty goblins.

"We even get to share a bedroom," said Kirsty.

She sat on her bed and bounced up and down. The room was pretty, with sunshine-yellow curtains and a vase of daffodils on the dressing table. The window looked out over the big garden of Olive House.

There was a knock on the door, and Rachel's mum came in with Kirsty's mum.

"Your dads have gone for an early walk and we're going to join the morning meditation class," said Mrs Walker. "Would you like to come?"

"Yes please," said Kirsty, jumping to her feet. "I want to try everything this weekend."

"Me too," said Rachel. "Josh made meditation sound amazing."

Josh was the Mindfulness Guide at Olive House. The girls had met him when they arrived the evening before.

"I thought so too," said Mrs Tate. "I hope I can be as calm and relaxed as Josh by the end of this weekend."

The meditation class was being held in the summerhouse in the garden. It was a sunny morning and birds were singing loudly in the leafy trees. When Rachel and Kirsty reached the summerhouse, they stopped in surprise. Josh was there, but he didn't look calm. His forehead was wrinkled with worry lines.

"Good morning, Josh," said Mrs Walker.

"I'm afraid it's not a very good morning so far," said Josh. "The chef is feeling too worried to cook breakfast, and there's something upsetting the yoga teacher, but we can't work out what's wrong. Everyone is anxious."

Read Ivy the Worry Fairy to find out what adventures are in store for Kirsty and Rachel!

Calling all parents, carers and teachers!
The Rainbow Magic fairies are here to help
your child enter the magical world of reading.
Whatever reading stage they are at, there's
a Rainbow Magic book for everyone!
Here is Lydia the Reading Fairy's guide to
supporting your child's journey at all levels.

(1)

Starting Out

Our Rainbow Magic Beginner Readers are perfect for first-time readers who are just beginning to develop reading skills and confidence. Approved by teachers, they contain a full range of educational levelling, as well as lively full-colour illustrations.

(2)

Developing Readers

Rainbow Magic Early Readers contain longer stories and wider vocabulary for building stamina and growing confidence. These are adaptations of our most popular Rainbow Magic stories, specially developed for younger readers in conjunction with an Early Years reading consultant, with full-colour illustrations.

(3)

Going Solo

The Rainbow Magic chapter books – a mixture of series and one-off specials – contain accessible writing to encourage your child to venture into reading independently. These highly collectible and much-loved magical stories inspire a love of reading to last a lifetime.

www.rainbowmagicbooks.co.uk

"Rainbow Magic got my daughter reading chapter books. Great sparkly covers, cute fairies and traditional stories full of magic that she found impossible to put down" – Mother of Edie (6 years)

"Florence LOVES the Rainbow Magic books. She really enjoys reading now" – Mother of Florence (6 years)

The Rainbow Magic
Reading Challenge

Well done, fairy friend – you have completed the book!
This book was worth 10 points.

See how far you have climbed on the
Reading Rainbow opposite.

The more books you read, the more points you will get,
and the closer you will be to becoming a Fairy Princess!

Do you want your own Reading Rainbow?
1. Cut out the coin below
2. Go to the Rainbow Magic website
3. Download and print out your poster
4. Add your coin and climb up the Reading Rainbow!

There's all this and lots more at
www.rainbowmagicbooks.co.uk

You'll find activities, competitions, stories, a special
newsletter and complete profiles of all the
Rainbow Magic fairies. Find a fairy with your name!